WHEN THE
RAIN SINGS

Project Director: Terence Winch, NMAI

Project Manager: Alyce Sadongei, NMAI

Photo Editor: Lou Stancari, NMAI

Research: Susan Secakuku, NMAI

Wordcraft Circle Liaison: Lee Francis

Editor: David Gale, Simon & Schuster

Designers: Anahid Hamparian and Lee Wade, Simon & Schuster

SIMON & SCHUSTER BOOKS FOR YOUNG READERS

An imprint of Simon & Schuster Children's Publishing Division

1230 Avenue of the Americas, New York, New York 10020

All rights reserved including the right of reproduction in whole or in part in any form.

SIMON & SCHUSTER BOOKS FOR YOUNG READERS is a trademark of Simon & Schuster.

The text for this book is set in 12-point Perpetua.

Printed in Hong Kong

10 9 8 7 6 5 4 3 2 1

Library of Congress Cataloging-in-Publication Data

When the rain sings : poems by young Native Americans / National Museum of the American Indian, Smithsonian Institution.   p.   cm.

Includes indexes. Summary: A collection of poems written by young Native Americans, inspired by or matched with photographs of artifacts and people from the National Museum of the American Indian. ISBN 0-689-82283-9 1. Indians of North America—Antiquities—Juvenile poetry. 2. Children's poetry, American—Indian authors. 3. Children's writings, American. 4. American poetry—20th century. 5. Youths' writings, American. [Indians of North America—Poetry. 2. American poetry—Collections. 3. Children's writings.] I. National Museum of the American Indian (U.S.)

PS591.I55W48 1999   811'.540809282'08997—dc21

98-31784

FRONT COVER: Hopi *Pahlikmana* (butterfly) katsina *tihu* (doll). Oraibi, Arizona. Height 37.5 cm. Photo by David Heald. 9.990

BACK COVER: Navajo hide doll. New Mexico. Height 58.75 cm. Photo by Gina Fuentes-Walker. 21.1986

FIRST EDITION

WHEN THE RAIN SINGS

Poems by Young Native Americans

National Museum of the American Indian,

Smithsonian Institution

◆◆ in association with ◆◆

Simon & Schuster Books for Young Readers

Contents

Cochiti—Kiowa

Tohono O'odham

Foreword

"I can feel the rhythm of a people/in the voices of the children," writes sixteen-year-old Patrick Lewis-Jose in "In the Rain," one of the center-piece poems of this collection. I think many readers will be as startled as I was at the range and quality of work in this anthology, at the ways in which young Indian writers give such fresh and eloquent voice to the joys and sorrows that fill all of our lives. There are lines here that only a young person could come up with:

Tsistsistas (Cheyenne) bonnet storage case, *late 19th century. Length 57.8cm. 2.8777*

". . . I'm a rough/and tough buffalo/and I am really cool, too" (Dewayne S. Mix, "The Buffalo Ran Away") or "Hey! This is my great-grandpa" (James Haggerty, "Untitled"); there are others, however, that embody a timeless wisdom that knows no age—as in the three powerful and accomplished poems by Vena A-dae Romero.

Perhaps drawing inspiration from the influential and compelling example of Native American oral tradition, contemporary Indian writers have made an increasingly significant place for themselves in the current literary landscape.

This anthology indicates that those advances show no signs of letting up. From the facility with rhyme evident in "Manido Mashkimod" (Rainbird Winters) and "The Ancient Doll" (Daisha Jim) to the technical dexterity of Kimberly Eagle Bull's "Stormfear," with its densely packed images that effortlessly mix abstraction with intense emotion, these young poets are clearly comfortable reconstructing a Western art form into a means of Native expression.

An interaction takes place in this book between the poets and objects from the National Museum of the American Indian. This kind of dialogue is of the utmost importance to us at NMAI, for not only does it help us to understand our own collection better, it also restores recognition of the life that we believe inhabits our objects.

These poems take us into the heart of Indian Country, and spare us neither the pleasure nor the pain of Native life today. There are poems of pride and anger, and of exultation in the glories and joys of cultural traditions. There are poems of loss, reminding us that young people are no strangers to the human condition, and that life in many Indian communities can be harsh and unforgiving. *When the Rain Sings* truly captures all the nuances of "the song of a culture" ("In the Rain").

—W. Richard West, Director
National Museum of the American Indian

(Southern Cheyenne and member of the Cheyenne and
Arapaho Tribes of Oklahoma)

About Wordcraft Circle and This Book
Following the Word Trail into the Future

The Wordcraft Circle of Native Writers and Storytellers
seeks to ensure that Native
voices—past, present, and
future—are heard through-
out the world. From its beginning in 1992 at the close of
the first Returning the Gift
Festival, Wordcraft has found
its purpose in the Native
American tradition of giving
back to others in response to
the blessings, the gifts, that
have been received. For those
involved in Wordcraft Circle, it
means giving the gift of experience to help others hone their
skills in the art of storytelling.

Kachinas, *1964. J. Michael Byrnes
(b. 1938; also known as Kyash Petrach;
Hofyee; Hotyee), Acoma–Laguna–Sioux.
Watercolor, ink on board, 126.25 x
101.25 cm. 23.7629*

From the start, Wordcraft's vision has centered on linking
established Native writers with those less experienced. During
an initial one-year commitment, the seasoned writers help the
beginners refine their work and learn all they can about the art of
writing. That linking continues, and has inspired a variety of activ-
ities, including workshop conferences throughout the country.

The Wordcraft vision also gave rise to the publication of the journal *Moccasin Telegraph*, a showcase for the work of beginning and emerging Wordcraft writers. In 1996, we expanded onto the Internet with our own Web site (www.teleport.com/~prentz/wordcraft.html), featuring an electronic version of *Moccasin Telegraph*. That same year also saw the publication of *Reclaiming the Vision—Past, Present and Future: Native Voices for the Eighth Generation* (Greenfield Review Press), which I edited with Abenaki storyteller James Bruchac. Thanks to a grant from the W. K. Kellogg Foundation, copies of this anthology, which brings together poetry and prose of novice and acclaimed Native writers, were donated to the libraries of every school funded by the Bureau of Indian Affairs (BIA).

One of the people inspired by *Reclaiming the Vision* was Joanne Sebastian Morris (Sault Ste. Marie Chippewa), director of the Office of Indian Education Programs (OIEP) at BIA. She urged all BIA-funded schools to join in a partnership with Wordcraft Circle to work with Native students on their writing, storytelling, and public-speaking skills. More than 250 Native students from these schools, who ranged in age from five to eighteen, became involved in this program, which we call the "Mentoring Initiative." The student writing that came out of this collaboration was marked by notable talent and ambition. Those of us involved in the project thought that these young and gifted voices needed to be heard far and wide. The only question was how to make that need become reality. *When the Rain Sings* became one of the answers to our question.

In the fall of 1996, during a conversation with Alyce Sadongei at the Smithsonian Institution's National Museum of the American Indian (NMAI), the topic of publishing student writing from the Mentoring Initiative came up. Alyce, Terence Winch (NMAI's Head of Publications), their colleagues Susan Secakuku, Lou Stancari, and Ann Kawasaki, and I met to discuss this proposal. We decided to circulate pictures of NMAI objects and archival photographs to student writers at Indian grade schools and high schools all over the country, and to ask them to write in response to these visual works. The students from a particular sovereign Native nation would respond to works identified with their tribe (a few of our young writers, however, chose to write about objects from culture groups other than their own). Later in the process, when we received some wonderful poetry not written in response to NMAI photographs, we surveyed works from the museum's collection to find good matches for these poems. We wanted a book that would be a dialogue between the visual and verbal, with both dimensions thereby enhanced. (Please note: ages of students are as of time of composition.)

An initial "cut" of all the work submitted was made by a group of Wordcraft Circle mentors, whose selections were then reviewed by me and the NMAI staff, with additional help from Wordcrafters Kent P. Blansett (United Keetocwah Band of Cherokee) and Molly Senior (Lenape), an intern with NMAI at the time. From the start, we were excited by the quality of the work the students produced. The only painful part of the process was not being able to include everything.

When the Rain Sings presents the heart-songs of the youth of Native America. It has been inspiring for all of us involved to get such a real and tangible sense of the wealth of creative talent among young Indian writers. Anyone interested in the cultural life of Native Americans will, I believe, be deeply touched by the words from the young hearts found among these pages.

—Lee Francis, National Director
Wordcraft Circle of Native Writers and Storytellers
(Laguna Pueblo)

Introduction
Native Necessity

Stone mortar carved to represent an animal.
Vicinity of the Dalles, Wasco County, Oregon. Length 21.9 cm. 19.337

The strongest voices in contemporary Native poetry are those rooted in community. Neither the difficult landscape of the reservation nor the impact of urban relocation has diluted the strength of oral literature, which endures through new forms. Many contemporary poets speak from the power of oral tradition when they return to the primary sources of knowledge—their villages and tribes. This significance of connection to community holds true for the young people whose work appears in *When the Rain Sings*. As poets of their communities, they help "remember" their cultural bodies—regenerating language and ceremony by investigation through language arts. In that sense, these poems are vital and innocent forays into our memories, fresh from tears and the rhythms of sorrow and joy that resonate in communities in transition.

The specificity of location and language is immediately apparent in these children's works. It is a pleasure, for example, to see a student use his Lakota name, Cokata Aupi (Cho-kha-tah-ah-oo-pi). His poem, in its repetitions of "Pine Ridge" alternating with his line-by-line narrative of ration day, is songlike and reminiscent of older Lakota works that are part of the living literature of his world. His last two sentences reiterate the tenacity of indigenous people: "But someday our children will carry on, / Pine Ridge / And our beautiful culture will never be gone / *Ma Lakhóta!*" This poem, like many others in *When the Rain Sings*, draws its strength from community life and memory.

It is not surprising that the writings of the young people in this book should be so clearly marked by their experience. Native arts are rooted in the belief that people are required to learn how to live in a specific environment, and through maintenance of crafts and skills—through the vocalization of one's own song—they learn to benefit and to invigorate not only their communities, but the earth itself. Our first song, as Diné (Navajo) singer Arlie Neskahi says, begins at birth with the first draw of breath.

This book presents not only literary works, but also cultural artifacts from the collection of the National Museum of the American Indian. As indigenous people responding to works of cultural significance, the writers of these texts are inseparable from cultural wisdomkeepers of two or more generations ago, when most of the artifacts shown in this book were still in the hands of their own people. Because there is so close a relationship between poem and object in this anthology, it is important to understand some truths about the nature of indigenous artifacts.

Notwithstanding exterior forces and enforced change, indigenous communities regard their art forms as documents, as works that store valuable knowledge. Native art—including objects, ceremonies, and such pre-colonial books as the Wallam Olum, the wampum belts of the Haudenosaunee, and the Aztec Calendar—held information that demonstrated our link to the environment from one generation to the next.

Stories and objects are ways of understanding one's place within the earth's benevolence, of learning about past hardships, of tracking the place of self and family in the infinite cosmos. Master artists were not supreme beings, but fluid connectors to the life force around them. Objects carry stories and bring information from their makers. New investigations of Navajo textiles, for example, show that certain rugs made for personal use are mnemonic artifacts—ceremonial and healing songs are incorporated into the textiles' designs by the weavers for the singers.

The record of a particular event in the life of the weaver, for example, could be incorporated through the use of special materials such as small pieces of feathers. Sometimes stories also jump boundaries, and the artist becomes a carrier between cultures. A Haida artist, for instance, once explained to me that his jewelry relied on metalwork knowledge originally acquired from the middle Americas. As he showed me his bracelets, he told a story of his son falling out of a canoe as a small child, and an older woman jumping into the frigid waters to rescue him. The woman described the rescue, and the artist made a bracelet of the experience. It is, then, quite appropriate for *When the Rain Sings* to link artifacts and stories, to present a conversation between poets and objects.

When Patrick Lewis-Jose writes, "It's the last drop of a refreshing / drink from the spring of / continuance and all that is left / is but a drop of remembering. / Some say the spring will fill / again from the depths of / Mother Earth," he reflects an understanding of the ways in which environment and the life of his community are intertwined. The poems and objects of indigenous people acknowledge the interconnection between humans and their environment. In the Plateau culture I am most familiar with, for example, salmon taught us about cycles—replenished by prayers of gratitude, the salmon people knew of our high regard, and we knew salmon as returning relatives. Hub after hub of commerce connected and twirled. Knowledge exchanged hands.

Much of that knowledge is embedded in metaphor and imagery, as is so apparent in Daisha Jim's "Burning Land": "Rocky white mountains / On top of the world / Humans walking to the sky / Flowers watching." As one looks at indigenous literature and ceremonies, the power of imagery as a means of memory retention is apparent. If a person was able to "make something," be it a poem or a basket, he or she would never be poor, and participation in the ceremony assured that no one would go hungry. It was only if we were song-poor or silent that we became impoverished.

But to own this gift, this ability to make things, is also to assume some burdens. Native literature comes with enormous responsibilities to tell the story or sing the song correctly. One flaw in a series of chants will stop a ceremony. This is a daunting mantle for a younger generation to wear, yet the poems of these students are indications that there is a vigorous need to locate, collect, and exchange works among our population. The poets in *When the Rain Sings* have entered into the Native literary tradition, one that is not always evident in the work customarily offered for public consumption or taught in mainstream classes on Indian writing. This alternative world view, this indigenous tradition, remains obscured from most audiences, simply because of lack of education.

I value the words of these students, for they go beyond an elite system of Western universality—talking to God or gods, flying, and making peace, these young emissaries of goodwill bring fresh insight to the oversimplified image of indigenous Americans. As Americans and apprentice wisdom-keepers of Native tradition, the students are a bridge connecting the past and present. So full of self-knowledge, health, and expressive designs of their own making, these young people and their poems articulate the future of our communities.

—Elizabeth Woody

(Confederated Tribes of the Warm Springs Reservation of Oregon)

Acknowledgments

All of us at the National Museum of the American Indian (NMAI) are very grateful to the young contributors to this collection, and to their parents and teachers as well. Because we received many more poems than could be accommodated in this book, we also want to acknowledge and thank those young writers whose works don't appear in these pages. Their time will come, too.

This project is the first collaboration between NMAI and Wordcraft Circle, the national organization of Native writers and storytellers. Joining forces with Wordcraft greatly facilitated our ability to work closely with a number of Native communities and schools throughout the country, precisely the kind of exchange we seek to foster at the museum. We must single out Dr. Lee Francis, Wordcraft's executive director, for special thanks. A poet and scholar himself, Lee brought his legendary energy and knowledge to the project. In these efforts he was ably aided by Kent P. Blansett, Wordcraft's treasurer. We were also fortunate in being able to enlist the formidable talents of Elizabeth Woody, one of the most respected voices among contemporary Native poets, to help us put the book in a larger context.

From the NMAI staff, I want to thank Alyce Sadongei (Kiowa–Tohono O'odham), our former training coordinator, and Terence Winch, Head of Publications. Poets both, they worked closely with each other, and with Dr. Francis, to make the difficult choices regarding what to include in

When the Rain Sings. Lou Stancari, photo editor with the Publications Office, shouldered much of the organizational burden the book involved with his usual dedicated persistence, just as editor Ann Kawasaki brought her trademark skills to bear on a multitude of administrative tasks. Susan Secakuku (Hopi), training program assistant, graciously helped with research, while Pam Dewey, Head of Photo Archives, and her staff provided the excellent illustrations you see herein. Finally, we owe much to David Gale, of Simon & Schuster Books for Young Readers, for his patience and support, and to his colleague Anahid Hamparian for her wonderful design.

—W. Richard West

Ojibwe

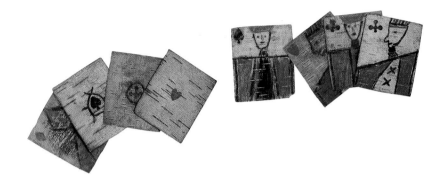

Ojibwe (Chippewa) birchbark playing cards. *5 x 6.25 cm each. 7.811*

Somewhere Deep Inside

Somewhere deep inside you
There is a feeling of love.

As you feel it, it grows stronger
And stronger
For the person you love.

It is just a great big feeling inside.

But one day you open your mouth
And say

I love you.

—Angela Cornelius *(Oneida Tribe of Wisconsin)*
Grade 6; age 12; Circle of Nations School, Wahpeton, North Dakota

Bad Luck
(The Life I Wish I Never Had)

The cruel world that I live in
     a mother with diabetes
         still searching for a cure
     a father close to cancer
         still smokes and can't stop
     a sister with asthma
         still a deep smoker to this day
     a brother with a learning disability
         and still fighting to learn more.

Soon enough the time will come
When they all step into another world
And a time will come
When I go home to my family
And someday that will be the end of us
Until the dawn of good luck comes.

—**Kelly Ahles** *(Chippewa)*
Grade 6; age 12; Circle of Nations School, Wahpeton, North Dakota

My Song

When I hear the old women
Telling of heroes
Telling of great deeds
Of ancient days
When I hear them talking
Then I think within me
I too am one of those.

When I hear the people
Praising great ones
Then I know that I too
Shall be esteemed
I too, when my time comes
Shall do mightily.

I love this
That is why I wrote this
For the Chippewa Indians.

—Kimberly Eagle Bull
(Oglala Lakota)
Grade 6; age 12 Circle of Nations
School, Wahpeton, North Dakota

Ojibwe (Chippewa) bandolier bag.
Beaded cloth. 108 x 33.6 cm. 20.268

4

Manido Mashkimod
(Spirit Bag)

A bandolier bag was from long ago
And is still used these days
It can be used in many different ways.

In history it was used in celebration
It is still very ceremonial
Throughout the Ojibwe Nation.

The traditional people wear these
When they dance
It bounces as they twirl and prance.

—**Rainbird Winters** *(Lac Courte Oreilles Ojibwe)*
Grade 6; age 12; Lac Courte Oreilles Ojibwe School, Hayward, Wisconsin

Ojibwe (Chippewa) cradleboard with painted and incised designs.

Michilimackinac region 24.2019

Empty Cradleboard

I hold in my hands
Something I needed
Once in my dream:

Sitting on a bench
With a child
Not mine
But like me
In so many ways
Alone without love
And held the baby
In my arms

Soon I had to go
I didn't know where
But I knew it was home
I had to take the child
The journey was long

I had a vision
I saw a cradleboard
For the baby
That was then mine
I knew the love I had to give
To receive the same
From this little one
So I made a gift
To give to my child
Not mine in birth
But in vision

I hold in my hands
A cradleboard
Knowing it is empty
Still I wonder
What happened to the baby
The one that should be
My mother

—**Millissa Alger** *(Mille Lacs Band of Ojibwe)*
Grade 9; age 15; Nay Ah Shing School, Onamia, Minnesota

Atikinaagan
(Cradleboard)

A cradleboard is used to hold a small baby
to let him fall asleep
It's like a mother hugs to hold him tight
to help him stop his weeping
He is observing everything around
both big and small
from the tiny little squirrel
to a tall oak tree

Eventually the baby will grow
too big to fit
but still the mother's love
will never end.

This cradleboard is sacred
used all the time
He feels so safe
and his heart beats with a lovely rhyme.

—**Rainbird Winters** *(Lac Courte Oreilles Ojibwe)*
Grade 6; age 12; Lac Courte Oreilles Ojibwe School, Hayward, Wisconsin

Ojibwe (Chippewa) man. *P18204*

I Look at You

I look at you and my mind drifts back to
    A time of peace and honesty
    A time of honor
    A time when all our people
        spoke our Native language
        and were proud to wear
        eagle feathers and beads.
    A time of dancing and giving thanks
        for all that Mother Earth
        gave our people:

        buffalo that roamed the grasslands
        fish that swam in clear blue rivers and lakes
        trees that our canoes were made from
        horses our people rode
        natural spring water pure and cool
        berries, roots, and bulbs, grown in rich soil
        rocks people used to tan hides
        stones our people used for arrow tips
Then I wish our people had that time again
    A time of peace and honesty
    A time of honor.

—**Kelly Hill** *(White Earth Minnesota Chippewa, Mississippi Band)*
Grade 10; age 16; Nay Ah Shing School, Onamia, Minnesota

Untitled

Hey! This is my great-grandpa.
He is old and wise and an old Chippewa man.
He fought the great wars and was wounded.
He loves me—his grandchild.
So I make a wish
To see my great-grandfather.
He dances with me and we pray
with one another
And we wear our feathers
to honor the eagle
And we wear our flowers
for medicine and prayers
So lend us your prayer
So we may pray for you.

—James Haggerty *(Turtle Mountain Chippewa)*
Grade 6; age 12; Circle of Nations School, Wahpeton, North Dakota

Lakota

Oglala Lakota camp scene, *ca. 1890. Pine Ridge, South Dakota. P22851*

Ration Day

We camped around the fort,
Pine Ridge
While the agent made his report,
Pine Ridge
You promised our rations,
Pine Ridge
Being Indian was not in fashion,
Pine Ridge
You tried to take away our pride,
Pine Ridge
Our sacred ways we had to hide,
Pine Ridge
But someday our children will carry on,
Pine Ridge
And our beautiful culture will never be gone
Ma Lakhóta! *

—Cokata Aupi**
—Quinton Jack-Maldonado
(Sicangu [Rosebud]–Oglala [Pine Ridge])
Grade 9; age 16; Little Wound Day School, Kyle, South Dakota

*"I am a proud Lakota!"

**Quinton signed off with his Lakota name—Cokata Aupi (Bring him to the center or in front of a gathering)—which was given to him at the age of three at a special naming ceremony. It is pronounced Cho-kha-tah-ah-oo-pi.

Representation of the Battle of the Little Bighorn, *ca. 1890, Oglala Lakota. Pine Ridge reservation, South Dakota. Painted muslin. 82.5 x 95 cm. 19.518*

The Fight

As guns shoot and arrows fly
Some of us do not even know why
We do not know how they came
We do not know who is to blame.

Now there are a lot of them here
The people know trouble is here
Our elders, women, and children suffer
We do not know the reason.

They put my people on a reservation
And then watch them from every station
My people, we get angry
We do not deserve this humiliation.

We ask them to leave us alone
But that is only the beginning of our mourning
They shoot us with guns
They think it is fun.

We fight back.
We do not deserve the bad.

—Danielle Dull Knife *(Oglala Sioux)*
Grade 7; age 14; Little Wound Day School, Kyle, South Dakota

Teton Lakota dance stick.

North Dakota. Carved and painted wood. Length 89 cm. 14.1566

Horse Dance Stick

Dance stick of painted and carved wood
There was a horse
A proud horse that was carried into battle
They went forth
Until they got killed.

Now it is a long time
And this stick is proudly, fiercely
Locked in a museum
If it is there I want to go see it
It is pretty cool.

I love horses
Horses are beautiful to ride
Horses are probably sacred
I love the colts
Horses are my life
I was raised on a farm
I rode them since
I was four years old.

—Angela Cornelius (*Oneida Tribe of Wisconsin*)
Grade 6; age 12; Circle of Nations School, Wahpeton, North Dakota

Lakota painted buffalo hide *(right)* **and detail** *(above).*

62.5 x 122.5 cm. 2.9360

Stormfear

When the wind works against us in the dark
And pelts with snow
The lower chamber window in the east
Whispers with a sort of stifled bark
The beast
"Come out! Come out!"
It costs no inward struggle not to go
Ah, no!

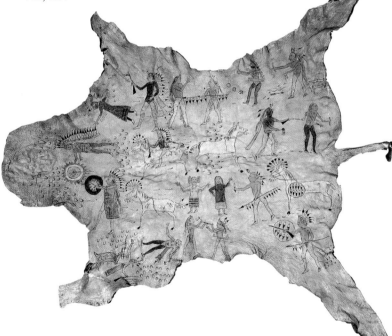

I count our strength
Two and a child
Those of us not asleep subdued to mark
How the cold creeps as the fire dies at length—
How drifts are piles
Door, yard, and road ungraded
Till even the comforting barn grows far away
And my heart owns a doubt
Whether it is in us to arise with day
And save ourselves unaided.

—Kimberly Eagle Bull *(Oglala Lakota)*

Grade 6; age 12; Circle of Nations School, Wahpeton, North Dakota

Omaha

If I Could See the Sky

If I was a bird
I would fly like an eagle
Through the sweet summer sky
All day long.

But one day I will fly
To the moon and the sun
All day long
I will not stop
Until I get to God.

Baby in a cradleboard
Riding safe
In the sky.

—Jillian Pappan *(Omaha Tribe of Nebraska)*
Grade 4; age 10; Circle of Nations School, Wahpeton, North Dakota

Omaha cradleboard. *Nebraska. Wood with brass tacks and beaded flap.*
Length 96.25 cm. 20.1373

Navajo

Navajo silversmith, *ca. 1906. Arizona. Photo by Karl Moon. N31720*

Ancient Ways

They're traditional.

They used to live in a hogan
> but now they live in a trailer.

They used to live in a village
> but now they live in a neighborhood.

They used to herd sheep
> but now they go to the grocery store.

They used to exercise
> but now they drive vehicles.

The father tells his daughter
> "Things are changing."

—**Elvania Toledo** *(Navajo)*

Grade 4; age 9; Atsa Biyaazh Community School, Shiprock, New Mexico

Untitled

Voices as silent as the winds
That blow through the piñon trees
And make swirls throughout
The hogan's earth top
Clinking sounds echo
Through the lonely hills

A child stands quietly
And watches her father
Make shapes into the silver
His eyes so wise and knowledgeable
The craft sent down
Through the many generations

And silently the girl stands
Eager to learn from him
Eyes so keen watching every move
Though the voices are silent
Only the wind blows throughout

I sat here quietly
To learn from my grandfather
As he once learned
When he was still my age

And in the future
My children and grandchildren
Will stand where I stand
And learn from me
Like I learned from my grandfather.

—Shawnetaiye Wynett DuBoise *(Navajo)*
Grade 11; age 17; Pine Hill High School, Pine Hill, New Mexico

Navajo hide doll. *New Mexico. Height 58.75 cm. 21.1986*

The Ancient Doll

She prays in the early dawn
sings the corn-grinding song
wears pink and red
Navajo bun on her head
turquoise jewelry and silver button
eats fry bread and mutton.

Her sheep graze
at the watery fountain
near her home
the beautiful mountain.

—**Daisha Jim** *(Navajo)*
Grade 4; age 9; Atsa Biyaazh Community School, Shiprock, New Mexico

Burning Land

Rocky white mountains
On top of the world
Humans walking to the sky
Flowers watching.

The Great Gods are sitting
in the clouds
"Walk faster, the land is burning,"
they say.
We pray for rain.

—Daisha Jim *(Navajo)*
Grade 5; age 10; Atsa Biyaazh Community School,
Shiprock, New Mexico

Navajo loom with unfinished textile; weaving tools.

New Mexico. Loom:113.1 x 104.2 cm. 19.3044

Cochiti–Kiowa

My Daddy Named Me A-dae

A-dae, everyone always called me.
Little, chubby A-dae
who wears her socks to her triple-folded knees.
Hulk-baby, Come Here!

Everyone held me,
pinched my cheeks, tried to make me smile.
My Daddy was my favorite,
My Daddy named me A-dae.

He had hands that wrapped around me,
folded over the embarrassment,
folded over the doctors who said I needed a diet.
I was too big for a three-year-old.

She's a Kiowa baby,
Kiowa babies are always big.
She ain't big neither, just filled with
    Indian Power.
She's gonna be the next Kiowa Princess,
    don't you know?

Kiowa beaded cradleboard,
ca. 1910. Oklahoma. Length 104 cm. 2.8380

A-dae, they called.
A-dae, A-night.
I always stood by him,
even when the shine leaked from his eyes.
When tubes and machines grew like vines.

Coma, the same doctor said.
No, just a little nap.
He hasn't responded for weeks.
No, dreaming is hard to break from.

He forgot how to make his tongue alive,
how to make his mouth grow,
how to make creatures push from his throat.
He remembered A-dae.

I said I love you, Daddy,
He shook his hand like he held a rattle.
A-dae. A-hope.
He whispered (through his skin),
Never drink like me, A-dae.

My daddy was my favorite,
especially when he said, A-dae, my Kiowa Princess!

—Vena A-dae Romero *(Cochiti–Kiowa)*
Grade 10; age 16; Albuquerque Academy, Albuquerque, New Mexico

Cochiti Pueblo family, *ca. 1920. Photo by Odd S. Halseth. N32987*

I Always Begin with
I Remember

I remember the time I learned to smile.
When laughter always tickled itself out of me,
When my little brother first saw light,
When I learned about happiness, the time our souls were one.

I remember the day Ba-ba* cried.
Vietnam, he said, a war . . . men became warriors.
A time the eyes became a little darker, a little older.
A time the rainbow hid behind the rain for many years.

I can remember the burn in my heart.
The pain of watching my daddy sleep in the arms of
    Mother Earth
when all those years he slept only in mine.
He said I was the only female he could trust.

I can remember the sunset.
The smile of the creator flexed so big across the sky,
the entire land was covered with happiness
that looks like an orange lace frosting.

I remember the day history almost disappeared.
The day Indian children's mouths were stuffed with English
    words,
and almost suffocated out of existence,
but they lay hidden in memory until it was safe, almost too
    late.
I can remember the stories of a thousand generations,

growing tall and green, bearing sweet yellow fruit,
eaten at the dinner table with Da-oo** and Ba-ba
watching the black leak out of their hair with each story.

I can remember the day my spirit began to rattle.
When memories encased in teardrops fell unto paper.
When the stories became waves, the silent words became
   medicine
I can remember the day memory became my hero.

—**Vena A-dae Romero** *(Cochiti–Kiowa)*
Grade 10; age 16; Albuquerque Academy, Albuquerque, New Mexico

Ba-ba in the Keres language means "grandfather."
**Da-oo* in the Keres language means "grandmother."

Bingo Bread

While the earth is webbed beneath frost and fog,
the women in brightly colored sweatpants
with sleep-drowned eyes and handkerchiefs wrapped
around their pillow-felt hair knock on Da-oo's door.
Da-oo herself wakes before the sun peeks
from behind the hills. The women glide in,
greeting each other in Keres and Da-oo melts in with them.

I make Folgers Crystals while gnawed by the keeper of sleep.
The aroma of hot caffeine, bad breath, and yeast swirls
in the air. The women's jiggling laughter calls up the sun
waking the world and gentle junipers. I watch their hands
work unconsciously, pounding and kneading the dough,
making immaculate round loaves.

These women are gifted in this art.
They work like efficient machines gassed by laughter,
gossip, and bingo. The women let their hands do the creating,
while gossip and words of bingo spill from their pinkish lips,
weaving this boring game into the tight threads of pueblo life.

The women now rest their arms and hands, but life and bingo
continue into the now warm morning. My mind, soaked with sleep,
only dreams of my warm pink bed, bingo daubers of bright oranges,

fluorescent pinks, and sky blues, and the bingo bread baking
    in the oven
until glorious brown while the women and Da-oo talk on.

—**Vena A-dae Romero** *(Cochiti–Kiowa)*
Grade 8; age 14; Albuquerque Academy, Albuquerque, New Mexico

Cochiti pottery figure of a man,
ca. 1880. New Mexico. Height 46.7 cm. 19.6726

Tohono O'odham

Tohono O'odham man gathering fruit from saguaro cactus, *1919.*

Near Blackwater, Arizona. N24484

Things I Would Miss About the Desert

The good things that I would miss
are the birds,
the owls, the hawks,
the eagles, the wolves, the cactus,
the chollas
the desert tortoise, the cool breeze,
the desert storms
when the ground is all wet.
I like to hear the coyotes at night
or to go out and sit in the desert
when there is a full moon.

—Angel Ramon *(Tohono O'odham)*
Grade 8; age 14; Marana Junior High School, Marana, Arizona

Being Indian

Being Indian is being proud
and happy for who you are.
Dark skin and dark hair
that make the white man stare.
Living in a village
with your relatives
making sure the desert still lives.
Keeping your head up
making sure no one
lets you down
'cause you're too proud
of who you are
'cause you're Indian.

—Dana Mathias *(Tohono O'odham)*
Grade 8; age 14; Baboquivari High School, Sells, Arizona

Akimel O'odham group making pottery,
1924. Onavas, Sonora, Mexico. Photo by Edward H. Davis. N24730

In the Rain

I can feel it sometimes in the
calm before the storm.
I can feel the rhythm of death
in my feet from the running.

And I can feel the fear in my
stomach as the dust surrounds
me and my feet hurt from
running.

I can hear the bullets fly overhead
like it was the Fourth of July.
And my ears hurt,
from listening.

And I can hear the women crying
and the babies.
Bullets are laughing and I can hear
the rhythm of death in the cries.

I was not there when it all
happened but my eyes
hurt from seeing and my
eyes hurt from crying.

When the rains come I am
blind but I can see it
all like it was only
yesterday.

It's the feeling you get
when you don't know
if you'll remember yesterday,
tomorrow.

And the tears from the long ago
times feel fresh from my eyes
as I recall what once
was.

And the songs of the storm
make me remember. Because you
can hear the old songs in
between the shouts of thunder.

The darkness comes close
like an old friend and offers
the only compensation for
years of degradation.

In sleep, dreams come and
dreams go. Sometimes we
forget and sometimes we
remember.

And my head hurts from
dreaming and trying to
remember and trying
to forget.

When the elders speak I can
hear the prayers from
long ago and those prayers
weep for remembrances.

I could see the history of a
people in the elders' eyes but
there are tears in their eyes and mine
sting from the pain.

Sometimes we forget the way
the song starts or the way
it ends. The song of a
culture.

When the rain sings and
we don't know what it means.
We hear the rhythm of bare feet
dancing and we can't figure it out.

It's the last drop of a refreshing
drink from the spring of
continuance and all that is left
is but a drop of remembering.

Some say the spring will fill
again from the depths of
Mother Earth.
And we will be full.

Some say the children will
once again bathe in the comfort
of culture and the seeds of heritage
sprout from their hearts.

Some say it will happen again,
that thing called culture and tradition.
The old ones say they can hear it
in the rain.

Maybe, when the bullets stop
flying, when the mothers, the
elders and the babies stop crying.
When we stop running.

If during the rain you can find
the words to the song of life,
the past, and tomorrow.
The song of a people, then maybe.

I can feel it sometimes in the
calm before the storm.
I can feel the rhythm of a people
in the voices of the children.

In the rain I can hear their new
feet dancing and remembering.
And in my heart the fear of not knowing
is covered with the hope,

of bare feet gripping the earth
in the rain.

—Patrick Lewis-Jose *(Tohono O'odham)*
Grade 12; age 16; Baboquivari High School, Sells, Arizona

From a book of drawings by Kiowa schoolchildren
(class of Mrs. Ida Fick), ca. 1895.
Near Anadarko, Oklahoma. Crayon and graphite on paper. 23.1620

The Sunrise

Sometimes I feel like
the sun rising over
the mountain looking
down on the
houses and
when I am
shining down
I am giving
a great big
smile.

—Juan Jose *(Tohono O'odham)*
Grade 2; age 7; Baboquivari High School, Sells, Arizona

The Wind Picks Up

The wind picks up
the cold air blows
the clouds bring
the loud sound
of thunder and the
flashing lightning.
The animals go to
their homes
and the people come
out and enjoy the rain.
The smell of the soil:
the rain falls just enough
to make a few puddles
then the rays of the sun
peek through the clouds
and the animals
come out and play
and soon
the sun is out
the puddles of water
and the sun create
a rainbow
that stretches across
the desert making
even more beauty.

—Rayna Two Two *(Tohono O'odham)*
Grade 8; age 14; Baboquivari High School, Sells, Arizona

Akimel O'odham woman and children,

1919. Alkali, Arizona. Photo by Edward H. Davis. N24559

Song

As I stand by my
grandma's mesquite
tree, I look at
Baboquivari Mountain, and
as the wind blows
across my face and
in my ears, I
hear my grandma
singing her I'itoi*
song. I smile and
when the wind stops,
I go and listen to my
grandma's low, soft
voice. And while
she sings it reminds
me of the wind starting
to blow again.

—Stephanie Vieyra *(Tohono O'odham)*
Grade 8; age 13; Baboquivari High School, Sells, Arizona

*I'itoi is the Elder Brother to the Tohono O'odham people. He lives on
Baboquivari Mountain and watches over them.

Akimel O'odham basket. *Arizona. Gen. Leonard Wood Collection. 23.1824*

Beautiful Flower
(In Memory of Winnie)

You were my flower
We shared the water that brought life into us
You were well rooted and stand strong
I saw in you strength
The storm came and the wind blew you
this way and that
Some petals fell off, but you were all right
The petals that stayed shined proudly
You were colored with laughter,
You and your crazy ways
As your stem became stronger
Your heart was lost
The soil you were in dried up,
No more color, no more water
The storm wore you out
Now you may rest
Know you are loved,
Know you will always be with me.

—**Julene Ramon** *(Tohono O'odham)*
Grade 12; age 17; Baboquivari High School, Sells, Arizona

Funeral

I'm trying to figure out why I'm hurting inside.
The bearers are all lined up, trying to be tough
    and not cry.
Everybody around has their head buried
    in their lap.
The night is cold and strangely still.
I'm afraid to look up at the big box lying
    in front of me.
People around seem to have no feeling but sad
    like the night.
The bearers line around the big box to pay their
    respects.
I close my eyes, take a deep breath, and
    start to cry.
The night seems to be long, not letting
    day come.

—**Colleen Francisco** *(Tohono O'odham)*
Grade 10; age 16; Baboquivari High School, Sells, Arizona

Akimel O'odham girls,

1920. Lehi, Salt River Reservation, Arizona. Photo by Edward H. Davis. N24542

Is It "I Am" or "My Name"

My name belongs to a dead white woman. How it got down
    to me?
I don't know. Josephine. Does not suit me. It has no meaning
But I am a meaning, a meaning for laughter
Like a feather of the eagle being patted over a child's body
    for blessing.

The child laughs.
I am a meaning, a meaning for strength
Like a father of the eagle being patted over my
    grandfather's body
        for blessing. My grandfather who is a warrior.
I am a meaning, a meaning of gentleness
Like a feather of the eagle being patted over my mother's
    body
        for blessing. My mother a heroine.
I am a meaning, a meaning of a birthmark.
Like a feather of the eagle being patted over my body for
    blessing. My name Spotted Feather.
        Not just my name it's who I am.

—**Josie Frye** *(Tohono O'odham)*
Grade 11; age 17; Baboquivari High School, Sells, Arizona

Divorce

I was sad
as a typhoon coming
closer and closer.
I didn't
have a heart
to hold on to.
It sounded like
too much peace and quiet.
It tasted like
a hot mint in my mouth.
It looked like
lightning beside me
when my mom and dad
got divorced.

—Davina Valencia *(Yaqui)*
Grade 4; age 10; Lawrence Elementary School, Tucson, Arizona

The Buffalo Ran Away

I wish I was a buffalo
My fur is brown and rough
as a torn-up tire.
I am strong as a tough man.
I am magic to joyful people.
I am all that, and I'm a rough
and tough buffalo
and I am really cool, too.
My eyes are as big as my body
and I'm faster than everybody else.

—Dewayne S. Mix *(Pima)*
Grade 3; age 9; Ocotillo Elementary School, Tucson, Arizona

Hopi

Hopi man hoeing corn. *Probably Arizona. N35274*

My Qu'ah

My *qu'ah** was nice
and he was a loving man
but he passed away.
I remember
How he used to carry me
when I was a baby
because I picture it in my mind.
His name was Wallace.
I remember the last time
I touched his hand.

—Tracy Tewa *(Hopi)*
Grade 3; age 9; Second Mesa Day School, Second Mesa, Arizona

**Qu'ah* in the Hopi language means "grandfather."

My Mom Is Gone

I miss my mom very much.
I guess God decided to take her.
We respected and loved her
but now she is gone.
I can't stop thinking about her
but sometimes
you just have to let things go.
When I am outside
I look way up in the sky.
It feels like she can see me
but I can't see her.
I have to let go of her
but I just can't.

—Corrina Poola *(Hopi)*
Grade 4, age 10; Second Mesa Day School, Second Mesa, Arizona

Creamware jar with painted decoration

made by Nampeyo (Hopi–Tewa). Arizona. 18.7533

Back in the Past

Back in the past
the Hopis used to live
in the Grand Canyon
in a real dark hole
that was the second world.
But it got flooded
and now we live on the mesas.
We used to live
in rock houses
until other people
that weren't our kind
came and built different houses
and it was never the same
in Hopi land.

—Kenneth Stewart *(Hopi)*

Grade 4, age 10; Second Mesa Day School, Second Mesa, Arizona

Clouds

Everytime I look at the clouds
they're always moving toward the east.
I was told that the great spirits
of the katsinas and our ancestors
are on those clouds
making their journey
and going back to the third world.

—Kris Holmes *(Hopi)*

Grade 6; age 11; Second Mesa Day School, Second Mesa, Arizona

Ute

Ute doll. *Colorado. Height 33.75 cm. 21.3022*

Leather Ute Doll

The doll is made of leather with its hide moccasins
Standing tall and proud with a beaded face
But no expression upon its face
Beaded pants of arches
With a beaded shirt made of leather
And a necklace to keep all the bad away
That's why the Ute made the doll
The one who made it kept the doll
Now that the bad stays away
The doll was given to a museum
To keep the bad away from all the Ute.

—Krystle Lee Cuthair *(Ute)*
Grade 6; age 12; Atsa Biyaazh Community School, Shiprock, New Mexico

Ute (Grand River Band) policemen. *N37109*

The Police

Long neat braids
Rest on their shoulders
with their big gold badges
and shiny boots
arrest drunks and murderers
lock them up day and night
see the prisoners
pull guns on anyone who disobeys
go from neighborhood to neighborhood
showing it is the police way
six Ute policemen can outdo twenty white men

—Krystle Lee Cuthair *(Ute)*
Grade 6; age 12; Atsa Biyaazh Community School, Shiprock, New Mexico

Indian Nations Represented

COCHITI

The Cochiti people are known around the world as masterful potters, silversmiths, and painters. Cochiti Pueblo, located in north central New Mexico, is the site of San Buenaventura's Day, a major annual feast day for this small community. Celebrated as a time of homecoming for the Cochiti, the day begins with morning mass and continues with a day-long Corn Dance.

HOPI

The Hopi call themselves *Hopítu* (or "peaceful ones"). The Hopi reservation is located in northeastern Arizona, with twelve villages located on the mesa tops of the Black Mesa plateau. The Hopi are famous for their katsina dolls (or *tihu*), which represent supernatural spirit-beings who bring rain, abundant harvest, and other gifts of life to the Hopi people. The katsina doll pictured in this section represents Butterfly Maiden.

KIOWA

The Kiowa are one of the most widely known peoples of the Plains region. The Kiowa Nation has preserved much of its traditional culture through stories, dances, and songs. Many styles of dance attire appearing at contemporary powwows are derivations of Kiowa designs. In recent years, there has been a resurgence by many tribes in the use of cradleboards, like the one pictured in this section. These beautiful but utilitarian objects symbolize the strong bond between children and their cultural histories.

LAKOTA

The Lakota, along with the Nakota and Dakota peoples, are often collectively called *Sioux*, derived from a name given to them by their traditional enemies. Several Lakota reservations are located in the Great Plains region; the Black Hills, spanning southwest South Dakota and northeast Wyoming, are considered by the Lakota to be a sacred area. Lakota dancers and musicians are active in the national powwow circuit, and the annual Lakota Nation powwow is attended by Native peoples from all over the world.

NAVAJO

The vast Navajo reservation extends across parts of New Mexico, Arizona, and Utah. Largest of all Native American nations, the Navajo are famous throughout

Utah. Largest of all Native American nations, the Navajo are famous throughout the world for their silverwork and intricately woven textiles. Navajo society is matrilineal, with women as the primary culture bearers for their people. Weaving knowledge and skills, representative of a complex set of cultural and spiritual values, are passed down on the woman's side of the family.

OJIBWE

The Ojibwe, also known as the Anishinabe or Chippewa, are part of the Algonquian language group. As members of the Three Fires Council, along with the Ottawa and Potawatomi, the Ojibwe resisted removal from their traditional homelands—the upper plains and midwestern states from Montana to Michigan. The elaborate bandolier bags for which the Ojibwe are noted are works of painstaking skill and technical mastery that often take as long as a year to make.

OMAHA

The traditional lands of the Omaha ("those going against the wind"), are located in northeastern Nebraska. Like many large Native American tribes, the Omaha Nation of approximately 6,000 enrolled members is run by a government consisting of an elected council and a tribal chairman. The Omaha are also frequent participants in national powwows. Omaha dancing and music, particularly warrior songs, have been influential in powwows throughout the Plains.

TOHONO O'ODHAM

The Tohono O'odham ("desert people"), also known as Papago, and the Akimel O'odham ("river people"), also known as Pima, are among the tribes who have never relocated from their traditional lands. Renowned for their popular basketry, O'odham basket-makers produce more basketry items than any other tribe in the United States. The familiar "man-in-the-maze" pattern (illustrated on the basket that opens this section) depicts Elder Brother preparing to journey through the life maze.

UTE

There are three Ute reservations, located in Colorado and in Utah, which derived its name from this tribe. The Ute have had a centuries-long tradition of extensive intertribal relations and trade with culture groups in the Southwest, Plains, and Great Basin regions. In particular, they are known for their basketry, including wedding baskets made specifically for sale There are three Ute reservations, located in Colorado and in Utah, which derived its name to Navajos. The doll pictured in this section was probably made by a parent as a toy for a child.

Object Information

p.1 and Ojibwe border: Ojibwe beaded bandolier bag. 103.5 x 26.7 cm. *4.8798*

p.13 and Lakota border: Santee Dakota painted parfleche. Devils Lake reservation, North Dakota. *18.1965*

p. 23 and Omaha border: Omaha wooden cradle-board with brass tacks and beaded flap. Nebraska. Length 96.25 cm. *20.1373*

p. 25 and Navajo border: Navajo *beeldléí* (blanket), 1880–90. Handspun wool and commercial yarn. 152.4 x 143.5 cm. *25.3708*

p. 33 and Cochiti–Kiowa border: Kiowa beaded bag, early 20th century. Oklahoma. 47 x 11 cm. *2.4378*

p. 41:Akimel O'odham basket tray. Arizona. Plant fibers, 24.8 cm. *11.415*

p. 61 and Hopi border: Hopi *Pahlikmana* (butterfly) katsina *tihu* (doll). Oraibi, Arizona. Height 37.5 cm. *9.990*

p. 67 and Ute border: Ute pipe bag with beaded decoration. Length 67.5 cm. *8938*

Photo Credits

Index of Authors/Titles/First Lines

Authors are in Roman • **Titles are in Bold** • **First lines are in** *Italic*